NICKELODEON

A Time to Share

D0095912

by Steven Otfinoski
illustrated by
Jim Durk

Simon Spotlight/Nickelodeon

New York   London   Toronto   Sydney   Singapore

**KLASKY
CSUPO**ᵢₙ꜀.

Based on the TV series *The Wild Thornberrys*® created by Klasky Csupo, Inc.
as seen on *Nickelodeon*®

SIMON SPOTLIGHT
An imprint of Simon & Schuster Children's Publishing Division
1230 Avenue of the Americas, New York, New York 10020

Manufactured in the United States of America

First Edition
2 4 6 8 10 9 7 5 3 1

ISBN 0-689-83383-0

Library of Congress Catalog Card Number 00-131525

Chapter 1

"I say, this is smashing isn't it, poppets?" said Nigel Thornberry to his wife, Marianne, and his daughters, Eliza and Debbie, as they watched a small herd of elephants drinking and splashing each other at a watering hole on Kenya's grassy savanna.

Marianne smiled. She had to admit that Kenya was turning out to be one of the best locations yet for their nature progam.

In the few days they'd been there, they had taken some excellent footage of zebras, lions, rhinoceroses, and giraffes.

"If only we could keep Donnie out of the picture," said Marianne. Every time she began to film any animals, Donnie joined them. Now he was frolicking with the elephants, who didn't seem to mind him splashing water on them.

"Out of the way, Donnie!" cried Nigel.

Donnie just grinned and resumed splashing.

"Oh, well," said Marianne. "We'll just have to edit him out later, I guess."

"Good idea," said her husband, fingering his bushy mustache. "It's a good thing we're here during the dry season."

"Why, Dad?" asked Eliza.

"Because all the animals come to the watering hole to drink when it's dry," explained her father. "All we have to do is sit here with our camera and wait for them."

"Well, you can sit here all day if you want, but I'm getting bored," said Debbie, Eliza's older sister. "Anybody for checking out the village?"

"Me!" cried Eliza, jumping at the chance to go somewhere with her big sister. "Can Darwin come too?"

Debbie made a face. "I suppose so," she said, "but he has to keep his distance. I don't want anyone seeing me walking around with a monkey!"

"Darwin's a chimpanzee, not a monkey!" said Eliza, defending her friend.

"Whatever," replied Debbie.

"Have fun, girls," said Marianne, before turning her attention back to the bathing elephants.

Soon the two sisters were in the village, strolling past tidy rows of huts with thatched roofs. Walking toward them were two teenage girls in colorful outfits.

"Wow!" cried Debbie. "You guys look cool."

"Cool?" said one of the girls, puzzled. "But it is so hot."

"She means she likes your clothes," translated Eliza.

"Thank you," said the girl. "My sister and I like your clothes too. You must be American tourists."

"Not exactly," said Debbie. "Our parents are here making a nature film for television."

"That's wonderful!" said the second girl. "Would you like to visit our home? We can tell you all about Kenya and offer you a cup of tea. Our country is famous for its tea as well as its wild animals."

"That sounds great," said Eliza.

"They weren't inviting you, dweeb,"

said Debbie in a low voice. "Anyway, you're too young to hang around with us big girls. Why don't you and Darwin check out the marketplace? I'll catch up with you later. *Much* later."

Before Eliza could say another word, Debbie and her new friends were walking down the street, talking and laughing.

"That's just like her!" cried Eliza. "Always ready to dump me when she finds someone her own age."

"It is not easy being the younger sister," said a gentle voice.

"Who said that?" asked Eliza. She turned around and spotted an elderly woman standing nearby.

"Uh, were you talking to me?" Eliza asked the woman.

"I certainly was," she replied. "I can tell you are a very special young lady."

"You can?" said Eliza.

"Would you like to come look at my wares?" she asked.

Eliza hesitated. She didn't want to buy anything from the woman, but her kindly smile made Eliza decide that she could trust her.

"All right," Eliza said, "but we can't stay very long."

Darwin was nervous as Eliza grabbed his hand. They followed the woman to a nearby grass hut. Out in front of the hut was a long wooden table with all kinds of things on it—bowls, spoons, masks, jewelry, and purses.

"Please sit," said the woman, pointing to two stools.

"Who are you?" said Eliza, curiously.

"I am the village elder," replied the woman. "I have lived many years and have seen many things. I have grown old, but I have also grown wise."

Eliza nodded.

"You are facing a problem with someone close to you," said the woman. "I have something that may help solve your problem."

With that, the elder reached into a small cloth bag on the table and pulled out the most beautiful necklace Eliza had ever seen. The string of colorful beads and shiny trinkets gleamed and glittered in the sunlight.

Darwin's eyes grew as wide as saucers as he stared at the necklace.

Eliza gasped. "It's . . . gorgeous," she murmured.

"Take it," said the woman, holding the necklace in her outstretched hand. "It's yours."

Chapter 2

Eliza stared at the shimmering string of beads.

"Oh, but I couldn't take it," she said. "It's much too precious."

"It is the custom of my tribe to give a gift to a visitor whom we think can use it," responded the village elder. "Take it."

Eliza carefully picked up the necklace. It felt cool in her hands.

"Put it on," the woman said.

Eliza did so and the elder held up a small mirror so she could see how the necklace looked on her.

"It's beautiful," said Eliza.

"You look like a princess," the elder said with a smile. Even Darwin was impressed.

"This necklace has belonged to many people over the years. It is always passed to someone who needs it."

Eliza looked up from the necklace. "You mean there's something magical about it?" she asked.

"We all make our own magic," said the woman mysteriously.

Eliza wasn't sure what the villager meant. But she felt it would be impolite to ask any more questions. Instead, she thanked the woman for her gift.

"You are very welcome," the woman said, rising from her chair. "And now I must say good-bye. Come and see me again before you leave."

"I will," promised Eliza. "And thank you again for the necklace!" Eliza and Darwin walked back out onto the muddy street. "What a nice old lady," said Eliza.

"I'm not so sure of that," Darwin said.

"Oh, Darwin," sighed Eliza. "Why do you always think the worst of people?"

"Because people can be bad," Darwin replied. "And I don't think you should have taken that necklace, Eliza."

But Eliza was too busy admiring the necklace and how it looked on her to hear anything Darwin said.

Together they returned to the Commvee where they found Debbie reading the latest issue of *Teenage Wasteland.*

"I thought you'd still be out with your new friends," said Eliza coolly.

"They had to go somewhere," said

Debbie. "But they invited me to a dance in the village on Friday night! Isn't that great?" As she looked up at her sister, Debbie's eyes caught a glint of light on the necklace. "Hey, what's that?" she asked.

"It's a gift from a new friend of mine," said Eliza.

"Someone gave you that necklace?" said Debbie. "Why would they do that?"

"Because she liked me," said Eliza.

A decidedly friendlier look came into Debbie's eyes. "Hey, sis, can you loan me your new necklace for the dance on Friday?" she asked. "It would really impress the boys!"

Eliza just stared at her sister. "You really expect me to loan you my necklace after the way you treated me this morning?"

"Oh, come on, Eliza!" cried Debbie.

"Look, I'll even introduce you to my new friends."

"You're only saying that because you want the necklace," said Eliza. "Keep your friends and your dance. The answer is no."

Debbie stared back at her sister. "You really are a dweeb, Eliza!" she cried and stamped out of the Commvee.

Eliza smiled and fingered her beads.

"That ought to fix her," she said. "It's just what she deserves."

Chapter 3

"Well, did you girls have a nice time in the village?" asked Marianne as the family sat down to dinner.

Eliza said nothing. Debbie turned her face away from the table.

"OOOOOOG, bhaaaaaPFFT!" exclaimed Donnie, gobbling down his food.

"Girls, is something wrong?" asked their mother.

"I'll say something's wrong," Nigel said,

sitting down at the dinner table. "Something is terribly wrong. We don't have a finish!"

"A what?" asked Marianne.

"A finish, an ending," explained Nigel. "All the footage we have of the animals on the savanna is quite nice, but we need something exciting, something really dramatic to end our film. I'm afraid the animals aren't being very cooperative."

"Maybe you should talk to them about it, Dad," said Eliza.

"Very funny," grumbled her father. "It's this dry season. The animals are so hot and tired they can barely move. Why couldn't we be here in the rainy season when they're more lively?"

Marianne frowned. She didn't need to remind him that he had said quite the opposite only that morning.

"We just have to be patient, dear," she

told him. "I'm sure we'll see something exciting before we leave. We do have three more days in Kenya."

"I certainly hope you're right," said Nigel, picking at his food.

"Brrrruppt!" cried Donnie, wiping his mouth with his hand and pushing his plate away.

Marianne suddenly noticed the necklace around Eliza's neck. "Where did you get that beautiful necklace, dear?"

Before Eliza could reply, Debbie suddenly stood up. "I just remembered I need to sort my shampoos. I'll finish eating later," she said.

Eliza stared after her sister. Marianne and Nigel looked at each other.

Eliza was the last one up the next morning. She liked her new necklace so much that she had worn it all night. Eliza found a note from her parents. They were on the savanna looking for a dramatic finish to their film and Debbie was in the village meeting with her new friends.

Eliza thought back to the night before and how upset her sister had been when she wouldn't let Debbie borrow the necklace for the dance. It made Eliza feel just the slightest bit guilty about how she had treated her sister.

"If I could make it up to her . . . ," she said as she and Darwin went for a walk.

"You could loan her the necklace," he suggested.

"Oh, no," she replied, touching the cool beads. "It's mine. It was a gift from the village woman and only I should wear it."

Just then she spotted a tall mango tree, filled with clusters of large, juicy red mangoes.

"I've got it!" she cried. "We'll pick

Debbie some mangoes from that tree. She loves fresh fruit."

"That's a nice idea," said Darwin. "But wouldn't it be easier just to buy some mangoes in the marketplace?"

"Oh, Darwin," said Eliza. "That's no fun. And these mangoes won't cost us anything."

"If you don't break your neck trying to get them," said Darwin, looking up. "That's an awfully tall tree."

"They say the ripest fruit is at the top," said Eliza. "Well, what are you waiting for?"

Darwin looked startled. "You don't expect me to climb that tree, do you?"

"I thought chimpanzees were natural climbers," Eliza replied.

"Maybe so, but this is one chimpanzee who's not about to risk his neck for you or your sister or anyone else," said Darwin, crossing his arms.

Eliza sighed. "Then I'll just have to climb the tree myself," she said.

"Now, Eliza, do be careful," said Darwin.

"Don't worry," Eliza said as she started up the tree.

"Don't look down, whatever you do!" Darwin called out.

As Eliza reached the highest branch, she spied a bunch of fat, ripe mangoes. They were just beyond her reach. She held the tree trunk with one hand and stretched out her other hand for the fruit. All at once she lost her grip on the tree and fell forward.

"Eliza!" cried Darwin.

Eliza landed hard on something big and furry. She looked up and saw the long, slender neck of a . . . giraffe. The giraffe bent its head down to where Eliza sat on its back and opened its mouth.

Eliza gasped.

Chapter 4

"And where did you come from?" the giraffe asked in a soft voice.

Eliza was too surprised to speak.

"Are you all right?" said the giraffe.

"Y-Y-Yes," she stammered. "I didn't know giraffes could talk or make any sound at all!"

"Nonsense," said the giraffe. "Of course we can talk! We just have tiny voices, that's all."

"It's a good thing you were here under the tree," said Eliza, looking down at Darwin. "That's a long way to fall."

"Maybe you'd like some help picking those mangoes," said the giraffe. "I wouldn't want you to fall again."

"That's very kind of you," said Eliza.

"It's my pleasure," said the giraffe.

The giraffe reached up with its long neck and gently plucked branches full of mangoes with its mouth and handed them down to Eliza.

Eliza missed one branch and it dropped to the ground below. A zebra who happened by, quickly picked up the cluster of mangoes and ate them hungrily. Then it looked up.

"Thanks," said the zebra. "Maybe you could throw down a few more. There's hardly anything left to eat down here."

The giraffe frowned. "Those mangoes

weren't for you," she said. "Go and find your own food."

Other animals were starting to gather below. Eliza saw a rhinoceros, a wildebeest, and an elephant. All of them looked tired—and very hungry.

"It's been so dry, even the tall grass we eat has turned brown," said the rhino. "Only you can reach the tender leaves and fruit that are left in the highest trees. Can't you share it with us, friend?"

"I'm sorry," said the giraffe coolly. "You'll just have to go elsewhere to find food. And don't call me 'friend.'"

Eliza was surprised to hear the giraffe speak like that. "You helped me," Eliza said to the giraffe. "Why can't you help them?"

"You're a human," said the giraffe. "You don't understand how it is in the animal kingdom. As a giraffe, I'm far above these other animals and I'll have nothing to do with them."

Eliza felt sorry for the other animals, but the giraffe wouldn't say any more. She went on picking mangoes and putting them in Eliza's lap, until her lap could hold no more.

"You'll have to jump off my back to get down to the ground," said the giraffe. "I'd go down on my knees to make it easier for you, but I'm afraid if I did, I might not be able to get up again."

"That's okay," said Eliza. "You've done enough already. Thanks so much for the mangoes!" Eliza tossed most of the fruit down to Darwin before jumping to the ground.

"Come and visit me again," the giraffe said. "It's so nice to talk to someone intelligent for a change."

Eliza said good-bye, and the giraffe ambled away to nibble on the tender leaves atop a neighboring tree. Darwin looked after her in disgust.

"She certainly is full of herself, isn't she?" he said.

"I guess she's so used to looking down on the other animals that she believes she's better than them," said Eliza. "It's too bad, because they sure could use her help."

Just then the rhino, the elephant, the zebra, and the wildebeest approached Eliza and Darwin.

"Let's get out of here, Eliza," whispered Darwin. "These animals look dangerous."

"Don't be silly," replied Eliza. "They look tired and hungry."

She gave each of them two mangoes which they quickly ate.

"Thank you, young lady," said the zebra. "You are very kind. Not like that selfish, stuck-up giraffe!"

"If only she could go hungry like us,"

said the elephant. "Then maybe she would change her tune!"

"That's just the way some animals are, I guess," sighed Eliza.

The animals wished her well, and she and Darwin returned to the Commvee. They found Debbie practicing a few dance steps by herself.

"I brought you some fruit, Deb," Eliza said.

"I don't want any of your smelly old fruit," Debbie shot back. "I just want that necklace for the dance tomorrow night."

"I'm sorry, but it's MINE," responded Eliza. "And I'm not sharing it with *anybody,* especially not you!"

Debbie stalked out of the Commvee.

Marianne entered from the kitchen. "Debbie told me about the necklace," she said. "Can't you let her have it just for one night? You know how much this dance means to her, Eliza."

Eliza wouldn't budge. "I'm sorry, Mom, but it's mine. Why should I give it to her when she treats me the way she does?"

"I know she isn't always very nice to you, Eliza," admitted Marianne. "But she's still your sister."

"If I could change that, I would!" said Eliza, stomping away angrily.

Marianne sighed. "What will it take to teach the two of them how to share?" she wondered out loud.

Chapter 5

It was Friday morning. Eliza and Debbie hadn't talked to each other for nearly two days.

Eliza could not stop thinking or talking about her necklace. Darwin was getting tired of it and wished they had never met the old woman in the village.

And Nigel was still trying to think of some way to give their Kenyan film an exciting ending.

"I think I've finally got it, dear!" he said to his wife as they trudged out onto the vast, dry, grassy savanna.

"What is it, Nigel?" said Marianne.

"Donnie can stir the animals up a bit," he explained. "He likes to get into the act anyway. Well, let's put him to work. If he can't get them moving, *nobody* can!"

Marianne had to agree with him. Donnie had an amazing effect on animals—and people.

Nigel called Donnie and the boy came scurrying over. "Nananadagaooow!" Donnie cried, giving Nigel a big hug.

"Isn't that nice," said Nigel, hugging Donnie back. "Come on, Donnie, we're going to find some animals."

Together, they all trudged out onto the vast savanna. Soon they spied a small herd of wildebeests not far away.

"Perfect!" cried Nigel. "Donnie, go out

there and get them moving!"

"Eeebettlewee!" cried Donnie, making a beeline for the wildebeests. Not having seen anything like Donnie before, the animals were so alarmed that they started to stampede.

"Oh, Nigel!" cried Marianne, looking up from her camera. "Look what he's done!"

"Oh, dear!" said Nigel. "I didn't tell him to start a stampede!" Suddenly he brightened. "But, I say, it does look exciting, doesn't it? We might as well take advantage of the situation and film it, eh, Marianne?"

Marianne looked again at the stampeding wildebeests and her eyes widened.

"What's the matter, dear?" said Nigel. "You're not out of film, are you?"

"No, but we may be out of luck," she said. "That herd is heading straight for us!"

"You're absolutely right," said Nigel.

"Maybe I can wave them to the right and you can film them as they run past."

Marianne knew that simply waving your arms was not going to stop stampeding wildebeests. She grabbed Nigel and pulled him behind a nearby baobab tree. The wildebeests thundered by, going right around the tree.

After the animals had passed and the dust had settled, Marianne came out from behind the tree. "That was close!" she exclaimed.

Nigel watched the wildebeests disappear into the distance. "Yes, but what a lost opportunity!" he said.

Donnie came running up to them, grinning from ear to ear. "Yammy! Yammy!" he cried.

Nigel hugged the boy. "Good job, Donnie," he said. "Too good, I'm afraid. It's back to the drawing board for us."

Donnie jumped up and down. "Ooo-ooo-pooh!" he exclaimed.

Chapter 6

While her parents were barely escaping a stampede, Eliza was with Darwin, talking to the plant-eating animals on another part of the savanna. They told her how scarce food had become and how hard it was to feed their young and themselves.

"If we don't find food soon, we will have to leave, Eliza," said the zebra. "Many of the old and young members of our herds may die on the journey."

"I wish I could help you," said Eliza.

"You can," spoke up the rhinoceros. "The giraffe likes you. Maybe you can convince her to share her leaves with us."

"I'll try," said Eliza, "but I can't promise anything."

Eliza left them with Darwin and found the giraffe by the watering hole, about to take a drink.

"It's good to see you again, Eliza," said the giraffe. "Isn't this heat terrible?"

"We don't mind it," said Eliza. "The Commvee is air-conditioned and we have plenty of food to eat. But the other animals aren't doing so well."

"If they weren't so lazy, they'd find food someplace else," grumbled the giraffe.

"But many of them may die looking for it," argued Eliza. "Couldn't you give them some of the leaves you pick from the tall trees?"

"Why should I?" replied the giraffe. "They don't even like me. Why, when I came here to the watering hole just now, they all scurried away. You'd think I had a disease or something!"

"But don't you see?" said Eliza. "The reason they don't want to be around you is because you won't help them. If you did, I'm sure they'd be your friends."

"Let me ask you something," said the giraffe. "If someone wanted the beautiful necklace you're wearing, would you just give it to them?"

Eliza was at a loss for words. The giraffe, not knowing it, had hit a sore spot.

"I—I don't know," she said weakly.

"Of course you wouldn't," said the giraffe. "It's yours and you want to keep it. The leaves are mine because only I can reach them. And I'm not going to share them with a bunch of stupid animals! Now if you don't mind, I'd like to take a drink. All this talk has left my throat dry as dust."

Eliza saw that nothing would change the giraffe's mind. She and Darwin started to walk away. Was she no better than the giraffe? Of course Debbie wasn't going to die if she didn't have the necklace for the dance, but why couldn't Eliza bring herself to share it with her?

Eliza lifted the glittering beads to the light. Somehow their sparkle wasn't so wonderful anymore.

"Can't you ever stop looking at that necklace?" Darwin said to her.

"Maybe I'm really seeing it for the first time," Eliza replied. "I think you were right, Darwin."

"Right about what?" asked her friend.

"Maybe I never should have taken the

necklace from the woman," said Eliza.

Suddenly they heard a loud splash. The giraffe had fallen into the watering hole!

"Help!" the giraffe cried. "I can't swim!"

Eliza looked around. She had to do something—and quickly!

Chapter 7

"Help! I'm drowning!" the giraffe cried.

Eliza told Darwin to stay by the giraffe while she rushed to where the other animals were resting near each other in the shade of a baobab tree.

"It's the giraffe," she said breathlessly to the animals. "She's fallen into the watering hole! She'll drown if you don't save her!"

"Let her save herself," said the elephant.

"But she can't!" cried Eliza.

"What's that to us?" the zebra said. "She didn't help us. Why should we help her?"

"That's right," added the rhinoceros. "She only has herself to blame for what's happened to her."

"All right," Eliza said. "If that's how you feel, I'll just rescue her myself!"

Eliza rushed back to the watering hole. "I don't think she can last much longer!" cried Darwin.

"Then it's up to us to save her," Eliza said.

"Save a 1,500-pound giraffe!" cried Darwin. "How on earth can we do that?"

Eliza said nothing, but yanked down a vine from a nearby tree.

"Here's what we'll do," she explained. "I'll swim out to the giraffe with this end of the vine. You tie the other end around the tree."

Darwin looked at the vine and then at the struggling giraffe. "Eliza, it'll never work!" he cried.

But Eliza wasn't listening. She dove into the water. Swimming to the giraffe, Eliza managed to slip the vine around her neck. Darwin struggled to get the other end around the tree.

"The vine's too short!" he yelled to Eliza. "It won't reach the tree!"

"Try harder!" cried Eliza, trying to stay out of the way of the struggling giraffe.

Hearing the commotion, some of the animals had gathered around the watering hole to see what was happening.

"Eliza's going to drown if she's not careful," said the wildebeest.

"Should we help her?" asked the rhino. None of the animals replied. Then the rhino added, "She did help us."

"You're right," said the elephant. "What are we waiting for?"

The elephant stomped over to the tree, took the vine from Darwin, and grasped it in his trunk. The other animals lined up behind him. The wildebeest grabbed the elephant's tail with his teeth. The zebra did the same to the wildebeest. Then the rhino asked Darwin to tie the end of the vine around his huge horn.

"Now, pull!" cried the elephant. As the animals pulled, the giraffe came closer to solid ground. It looked like a tug-of-war. Finally, after one last tug, the giraffe and Eliza lay exhausted and gasping alongside the watering hole.

"Eliza!" cried Darwin. "Thank goodness you're all right!"

Eliza smiled, and the giraffe sat up and looked around at the other animals.

"Thank you for saving me," the giraffe said quietly.

"Don't thank us," said the elephant. "If it weren't for Eliza we wouldn't have bothered. But I suppose we're glad you're all right too."

The giraffe turned to Eliza. "It looks like I need to thank you twice, Eliza," she said. "Once for saving my life . . . and secondly for showing me that it takes everyone working together to get through bad times. It's time I did my share."

All the animals nodded.

"From now on, my friends, I'm going to give you all the leaves you need until this drought is over," promised the giraffe. "And I'll try to make up for the terrible way I treated you."

The animals helped their new friend to her feet. Eliza started to leave.

"Come on, Darwin, I have someone I have to make up with too," she said.

Chapter 8

Eliza found her sister sitting outside the Commvee eating a mango. As soon as Debbie saw Eliza she swallowed the piece of fruit and looked embarrassed.

"I got hungry and decided to eat one of your mangoes after all," she said.

"That's okay," replied Eliza. "They were meant for you. And I have something else to give you."

Eliza took off the necklace and held it out to Debbie.

"I know now I was being selfish when I said no to you," said Eliza. "I may not have liked what you did to me, but you're still my sister."

Debbie looked at the necklace in her hands in amazement. "You're loaning me the necklace?" she asked.

"Not loaning," corrected Eliza. "I'm *giving* it to you. It probably looks better on you than me anyway."

Debbie tried on the necklace. Eliza grinned. "You look spectacular," she said.

"Oh, but there's no way I'll keep it," Debbie protested. "I've been doing some serious thinking too, sis. And it was pretty dumb the way I treated you the other day. I'll wear the necklace to the dance tonight . . . but only on one condition."

"What's that?" asked Eliza.

"That you'll come with me to the dance

and hang out with me and my new friends," said Debbie.

"That would be great!" cried Eliza, giving her sister a big hug.

Just then their father came rushing in. "Girls! Girls!" Nigel cried. "You won't believe what your mother and I have just seen!"

"Not another wildebeest stampede," said Debbie, rolling her eyes.

"No, no!" said Nigel. "This is far more extraordinary. Unique, really. We actually saw a giraffe pulling leaves from a tree and dropping them to the ground where the other animals picked them up and ate them."

"Maybe she's just a sloppy eater," said Debbie.

"No, I'm sure she knew exactly what she was doing," said Nigel. "She was sharing her food with the other animals in her community. I've never seen such cooperation between animals in the wild before. What a stupendous discovery!"

"Sounds exciting, Dad," said Eliza with a grin.

"The best part is that we got it all on film! Now we have just the right ending for our program on Kenya," continued Nigel. "By Jove, girls, we may win an award for this one. Wouldn't that be smashing?"

Eliza hugged her Dad. She didn't tell him that she already had her reward. She had her sister back.

Chapter 9

Nigel was so happy about his "discovery" that he decided they would all go to the dance at the village square to celebrate. Debbie wasn't thrilled to have her parents at the dance, but once she arrived she was quickly surrounded by her new friends. They were enchanted with her necklace. Some of the boys were impressed too.

Debbie kept her word and introduced

Eliza to her friends. The two sisters from the village taught Debbie and Eliza some dance steps. Eliza loved dancing to the pounding rhythms of the *ngoma* drums.

Even Nigel and Marianne joined in the dancing. "I say, this is cracking, Marianne! I haven't had this much fun since . . . since I don't remember when!" exclaimed Nigel breathlessly.

Suddenly there was a loud commotion at one end of the village square. Many of the dancers stopped to gather in a circle.

Eliza and Debbie joined the onlookers.

"Who is it?" said Debbie. "They must be super on their feet to cause such a scene."

Eliza peeked over someone's shoulder and started to laugh. So did Debbie. In the center of the circle, jumping up and down wildly, were Donnie and Darwin!

"We have never seen anything like this before," said one of Debbie's friends. "Where did your brother learn to dance like that?"

"*Please,*" said Debbie. "Donnie is *not* our brother! And I don't know where he learned to do anything."

Soon everyone joined in the twosome's wacky dance, imitating their steps. Darwin finally stopped dancing and stumbled over to Eliza.

"Darwin!" whispered Eliza. "I never knew you could dance like that!"

"Neither did I," said the exhausted chimpanzee. "But I don't know what came over me. Once I heard those pounding drums, my feet took on a life of their own. Oh, I do hope I don't get sick from all this overexertion!"

At the end of the night, Debbie returned the necklace to Eliza.

"Thanks, sis," said Debbie. "It made my last night in Kenya really special! And, uh . . ." Debbie paused before adding,

"I'm glad you hung out with me."

Eliza grinned as she gave her sister a big hug. Then telling Debbie that she would meet her back at the Commvee, Eliza rushed off with Darwin to the hut of the village elder.

"She's probably sound asleep, Eliza," said Darwin. "You'll wake her up."

But when they arrived at the hut a light was on. "I'm glad you're still up," Eliza said to the woman as she came to the door.

"Of course I'm still up," smiled the woman. "I saw you were having fun at the dance. And your sister, too. Now to what do I owe this visit?"

"I don't want to seem ungrateful," said Eliza, "but I've come to return your necklace."

"What's the matter?" the woman asked. "Don't you like it?"

"Oh, I love it," said Eliza quickly. "But I

can't keep it. It should stay here with you and your family. It, uh, taught me an important lesson."

"And what lesson is that?" asked the elder.

Eliza took a deep breath. "That it's more fun sharing what you have with others than keeping it all to yourself," said Eliza. "And in the end, family and friends are more precious than all the necklaces in the world."

The woman smiled as she took back the necklace. "You have learned a very valuable lesson, indeed," she said. "Now get some sleep. You are leaving our wonderful land tomorrow."

Eliza thanked her again and left with Darwin. "That old woman was really wise, Darwin," Eliza said. "You think we'll be as wise when we're old?"

Darwin frowned. "Speak for yourself,

Eliza," he said. "I'm quite wise enough, thank you. If only you would recognize that fact and listen to my advice more often. Then maybe you wouldn't get into so much trouble."

Eliza laughed and took Darwin's hand. Together, they headed for the Commvee in the soft moonlight that lit up the silent and beautiful Kenyan savanna.

Discovery Facts

Baobab Tree: A native tree that appears to be upside down. It can survive very dry conditions because its spongy trunk is capable of storing large amounts of water.

Kenya: A country on the east coast of Africa.

Mango: A juicy fruit, about the size of a large apple, that grows in tropical regions.

Ngoma (n-GO-ma): Large Kenyan drums, often made from hollowed-out tree trunks with cowhide stretched over the top.

Savanna: A broad, largely treeless plain covered with grass. More than two-fifths of Africa's total land area is savanna.

Wildebeest: Also known by its African name, gnu (*NOO*), this is a large antelope that lives on the savanna. It has long horns, thin legs, and a tail like a horse.

YOU CAN ENTER FOR A CHANCE TO **WIN A TRIP** FOR FOUR TO **NICKELODEON STUDIOS® FLORIDA!**

1 GRAND PRIZE:
A 3-day/2-night trip for four to Nickelodeon Studios in Orlando, Florida

3 FIRST PRIZES:
A Sony Playstation® system and a *Rugrats™ in Paris* Playstation game from THQ®

25 SECOND PRIZES:
A *The Wild Thornberrys* CD-ROM from Mattel Interactive

100 THIRD PRIZES:
A set of four books from Simon & Schuster Children's Publishing, including a *The Wild Thornberrys* title, a *Rugrats* title, a *SpongeBob SquarePants* title, and a *Hey Arnold!* title

Complete entry form and send to:
Simon & Schuster Children's Publishing Division
Marketing Department/ "Nickelodeon Studios Florida Sweepstakes"
1230 Avenue of the Americas, 4th Floor, NY, NY 10020

Name_____ Birthdate___/___/_____

Address_____

City_____ State_____ Zip_____

Phone (____) _____

Parent/Guardian Signature _____

See back for official rules.

Simon & Schuster Children's Publishing Division/ "Nickelodeon Studios Florida Sweepstakes" Sponsor's Official Rules:

NO PURCHASE NECESSARY.

Enter by mailing this completed Official Entry Form (no copies allowed) or by mailing a 3 1/2" x 5" card with your complete name and address, parent and/or legal guardian's name, daytime telephone number, and birthdate to the Simon & Schuster Children's Publishing Division/ "Nickelodeon Studios Florida Sweepstakes," 1230 Avenue of the Americas, 4th Floor, NY, NY 10020. Entry forms are available in the back of *The Rugrats Files #3: The Quest for the Holey Pail* (12/2000*), Rugrats Chapter Book #10: Dil in a Pickle* (11/2000), *The Wild Thornberrys Chapter Book #2: Two Promises Too Many!* (9/2000), *The Wild Thornberrys Chapter Book #3: A Time to Share* (9/2000), *SpongeBob SquarePants Trivia Book* (9/2000), *SpongeBob SquarePants Joke Book* (9/2000), *Hey Arnold! Chapter Book #1: Arnold for President* (9/2000), and *Hey Arnold! Chapter Book #2: Return of the Sewer King* (9/2000), and on the web site SimonSaysKids.com. Sweepstakes begins 8/1/2000 and ends 2/28/2001. Entries must be postmarked by 2/28/01 and received by 3/15/01. Not responsible for lost, late, damaged, postage-due, stolen, illegible, mutilated, incomplete, or misdirected or not delivered entries or mail, or for typographical errors in the entry form or rules. Entries are void if they are in whole or in part illegible, incomplete, or damaged. Enter as often as you wish, but each entry must be mailed separately. Entries will not be returned. Winners will be selected at random from all eligible entries received in a drawing to be held on or about 3/30/01. Grand prize winner must be available to travel during the months of June and July 2001. If Grand Prize winner is unable to travel on the specified dates, prize will be forfeited and awarded to an alternate. Winners will be notified by mail within 30 days of selection. The grand prize winner will be notified by phone as well. Odds of winning depend on the number of eligible entries received.

Prizes: One Grand Prize: A 3-day/2-night trip for four to Nickelodeon Studios in Orlando, FL, including a VIP tour, admission for four to Universal Studios Florida, round-trip coach airfare from a major U.S. airport nearest the winner's residence, and standard hotel accommodations (2 rooms, double occupancy) of sponsor's choice. (Total approx. retail value: $2,700.00). Winner must be accompanied by a parent or legal guardian. Prize does not include transfers, gratuities, or any other expenses not specified or listed herein. 3 First Prizes: A Sony Playstation system and a *Rugrats* Playstation game from THQ. (Total approx. retail value: $150.00 each). 25 Second Prizes: A *The Wild Thornberrys* CD-ROM from Mattel Interactive. (Approx. retail value: $29.99 each). 100 Third Prizes: A set of four books from Simon & Schuster Children's Publishing, including a *The Wild Thornberrys* title, a *Rugrats* title, a *SpongeBob SquarePants* title, and a *Hey Arnold!* title. (Total approx. retail value: $12.00 per set).

The sweepstakes is open to legal residents of the continental U.S. (excluding Puerto Rico) and Canada (excluding Quebec) ages 5-13 as of 2/28/01. Proof of age is required to claim prize. Prizes will be awarded to winner's parent or legal guardian. Void wherever prohibited or restricted by law. All provincial, federal, state, and local laws apply. Simon & Schuster Inc. and MTV Networks and their respective officers, directors, shareholders, employees, suppliers, parent companies, subsidiaries, affiliates, agencies, sponsors, participating retailers, and persons connected with the use, marketing, or conducting of this sweepstakes are not eligible. Family members living in the same household as any of the individuals referred to in the preceding sentence are not eligible.

One prize per person or household. Prizes are not transferable, have no cash equivalent, and may not be substituted except by sponsors, in the event of prize unavailability, in which case a prize of equal or greater value will be awarded. All prizes will be awarded.

If a winner is a Canadian resident, then he/she must correctly answer a skill-based question administered by mail.

All expenses on receipt and use of prize including provincial, federal, state, and local taxes are the sole responsibility of the winner's parent or legal guardian. Winners' parents or legal guardians may be required to execute and return an Affidavit of Eligibility and Publicity Release and all other legal documents which the sweepstakes sponsors may require (including a W-9 tax form) within 15 days of attempted notification or an alternate winner will be selected. The grand prize winner, parent or legal guardian, and travel companions will be required to execute a liability release form prior to ticketing.

Winners' parents or legal guardians on behalf of the winners agree to allow use of winners' names, photographs, likenesses, and entries for any advertising, promotion, and publicity purposes without further compensation to or permission from the entrants, except where prohibited by law.

Winners and winners' parents or legal guardians agree that Simon & Schuster, Inc., Nickelodeon Studios, THQ, and MTV Networks and their respective officers, directors, shareholders, employees, suppliers, parent companies, subsidiaries, affiliates, agencies, sponsors, participating retailers, and persons connected with the use, marketing, or conducting of this sweepstakes shall have no responsibility or liability for injuries, losses, or damages of any kind in connection with the collection, acceptance, or use of the prizes awarded herein, or from participation in this promotion.

By participating in this sweepstakes, entrants agree to be bound by these rules and the decisions of the judges and sweepstakes sponsors, which are final in all matters relating to the sweepstakes. Failure to comply with the Official Rules may result in a disqualification of your entry and prohibition of any further participation in this sweepstakes.

The first names of the winners will be posted at SimonSaysKids.com or the first names of the winners may be obtained by sending a stamped, self-addressed envelope after 3/30/01 to Prize Winners, Simon & Schuster Children's Publishing Division "Nickelodeon Studios Sweepstakes," 1230 Avenue of the Americas, 4th Floor, NY, NY 10020.

Sponsor of sweepstakes is Simon & Schuster Inc.